UNDER ALASKA'S MIDNIGHT SUN

DEB VANASSE

ILLUSTRATED BY JEREMIAH TRAMMELL

PAWS IV
PUBLISHED BY SASQUATCH BOOKS

Text ©2005 by Deb Vanasse
Illustrations ©2005 by Jeremiah Trammell
All rights reserved. No portion of this book may be reproduced or utilized in any form, or by any electronic, mechanical, or other means without the prior written permission of the publisher.

Printed in China
Published by Sasquatch Books
Distributed by Publishers Group West
14 13 12 11 10 09   6

Book design: Kate Basart

Library of Congress Cataloging-in-Publication Data is available.
ISBN: 1-57061-451-2 (hardcover) / 1-57061-422-9 (paperback)

Sasquatch Books
119 South Main Street, Suite 400
Seattle, WA 98104
(206) 467-4300
www.sasquatchbooks.com
custserv@sasquatchbooks.com

I can't sleep!
I won't sleep!
In fact, Mama says I don't have to sleep.
We're under the midnight sun.

We wait all winter
in the cold and dark
for summer's sunlit nights.
At last winter fades,
and we celebrate
the longest day of the year.

The sun stays up late,
and so will we,
enjoying the sun-soaked night.
But some will sleep,
like my brother Pete,
before midnight comes around.

Not me!
I'll run and
laugh and
play all night
under the midnight sun.

We skip through the meadow
where the fireweed grows,
where the fox sits high on the hill.
He turns and stares,
eyes blazing a dare,
unafraid in the midnight sun.

We cast our lines
in the sun-speckled creek.
Slippery salmon shimmer below.
One leaps with a splash,
fish-dancing at last,
having fun in the midnight sun.

We hide in the grasses
where the mama duck runs,
baby ducks trailing behind.
One circles around,
flapping wings up and down,
quacking loud at the midnight sun.

We pluck wild roses,
weave sweet-smelling crowns—
one for Mama, too.
She lifts her head high
as the Queen of Not-Night,
reigning under the midnight sun.

Pete stretches and yawns.
"Tired?" I ask.
He shakes his head to answer no.
But we all can see
he'll go to sleep
before midnight finally comes.

Not me!
I'm wide, wide awake
on the longest day of the year.

We pause for the moose
with her long, slow steps,
a little one by her side.
He twitches one ear,
and I creep close to see
if we'll be friends in the midnight sun.

We climb a hill
to the rat-a-tat-tat
of a woodpecker high in a tree.
Stay awake, he taps.
Midnight's coming up fast!
Don't miss out on the solstice sun!

We shield our eyes
and point toward the sky
where an eagle soars on the wind.
Her wings whistle a song
of creatures long gone,
a story old as the midnight sun.

Pete sits down
and rubs his eyes.
He lays his head in Mama's lap.
Soon he's fast asleep,
breathing slow and deep
as if it's any other night.

Not me!
I can't sleep!
I won't sleep!
I don't have to sleep.
It's the longest day of the year.

"Sit," Mama says,
"and rest awhile."
I crouch down in the cool green grass.
Out slips a yawn.
"You could lie down,"
she says, but I won't do that.

Mama rubs my head
and her eyes fall shut.
Soon she's sleeping, too.
I snuggle close,
and my eyelids close.
Just for a moment, I tell myself.

The sun's broad rays
stretch across the sky.
The mountains glow like fire.
Midnight arrives—
I can't close my eyes—
I've got to celebrate the light.

I stand,   I spin,   I dance

all alone
with the sun still shining bright.

Now I can sleep.
I will sleep.
In fact, I'll even
be happy to sleep
under the midnight sun.

Author's Note

In the far northern parts of the world, near and above the Arctic Circle, summer days are very long. For example, in Barrow, Alaska, the sun rises in May and sets eighty-three days later, in early August. During this time, the sun shines all through the night. People call it the *midnight sun*.

When the midnight sun is shining, people and animals stay active even at night. It's hard to sleep with so much light, but there will be plenty of darkness when winter comes. In Barrow, the sun sets in mid-November and doesn't rise again until the end of January, sixty-seven days later.

June 21, the summer solstice, is the longest day of the year in the Northern Hemisphere. All over the far north, people celebrate with games, races, and parties. Everyone loves to stay up late and enjoy the midnight sun.